Ark Angels
T.M.

Susie's Afraid of the Dark

Created and illustrated by
Joanne (Jodie) McCallum

Written by
Barbara Linville

©1989 Merchandising Development Corp.
in cooperation with McCallum Design Co.
Published by The STANDARD PUBLISHING Company, Cincinnati, Ohio.
Division of STANDEX INTERNATIONAL Corporation. Printed in U.S.A.
Library of Congress Catalog Card Number 89-062629

"Dear me," said Higher Ark. He was looking through his special telescope at the earth below. "Another little child needs our help."

"What's the matter, Higher Ark?" asked Angel Curious, tilting his kitten ears and whiskers forward.

"Yes, what's the matter, Higher Ark?" echoed Angels Cherish and Charity together, their little black koala eyes full of concern.

"It's little Susie Anderson," said Higher Ark. He put on his glasses and shook his head sadly. "She's crying again. Listen."

The Ark Angels got very quiet and listened with all their ears. "Oh," said Angel Cherish. "Susie needs our love."

"What can we do to help?" asked Angel Charity.

"Susie's afraid," said Higher Ark.

"What's she afraid of?" asked Curious.

Higher Ark sighed. "That's the sad part," he said. "She's afraid of just about everything. Cats and dogs and thunder and lightning and especially the dark. That's why she's crying now. Because she's alone in the dark."

"Are you going to send somebody to help her, Higher Ark?" asked Curious.

"Do you want to help?" Higher Ark asked back.

Curious dug his toe into the cloud and blushed. "I'm afraid of the dark too," he said sadly.

Higher Ark patted the kitten's head kindly. "Don't be sad, Little Friend. You're getting less afraid each day. Soon you won't be afraid of the dark at all. Just be patient. You'll come out all right."

"We need someone really brave," said Angel Cherish.

"Someone who can really *do* something," added Angel Charity.

Higher Ark nodded. "Yes, I think we'd better send for Angel Valiant," he replied. "He's the bravest little angel of all."

"Angel Valiant to the Higher Ark," he called through a long tube. And his words fell down, down, down the tube and finally rolled out the other end. And Angel Valiant heard Higher Ark say, "Angel Valiant to the Higher Ark."

So Angel Valiant began to go up-clouds. But it took him a long time. Because, though Angel Valiant was the bravest angel, he was also the smallest angel. In fact, Angel Valiant was a mouse—a twitched-nosed, scamper-footed, long-tailed mouse. Up, up climbed little Valiant over the humpy, bumpy clouds till he came to Higher Ark's office.

"You sent for me, Sir?" he said in quick little words that scampered as fast as his feet.

"Yes, Angel Valiant," answered Higher Ark. "I have a special job that only you can do. It's little Susie Anderson, you see. She's afraid of animals and lightning and thunder and the dark and even of her grandfather if he wears his glasses. Do you think you can help her?"

"Of course I can," replied Angel Valiant as he folded his arms confidently.

Higher Ark pushed his glasses further up on his nose and said, "You know that you will need to be different down there on earth so you won't frighten Susie even more?"

"Yes, I know," said Valiant impatiently. "I'm ready. Just bring on the halo dust and the down-cloud."

So Higher Ark called a down-cloud and little Valiant stepped onto it. Then Higher Ark sprinkled some halo dust over him and said,

Down to earth now you descend
To help our little frightened friend.

And immediately the cloud carried Angel Valiant down, down, down to the earth below. Down, down through the night sky and right down through the lights of the city. Down, down and into an open window of the Anderson house right into Susie's room and onto her bed. And as soon as Angel Valiant's foot touched Susie's quilt there was a little sparkle of halo dust as he turned into a soft and springy toy.

Now Susie had been crying softly in the dark, but suddenly she saw a little glow of light at the foot of her bed. "Oh!" she said. "What was that?" And she crawled out of her covers to see.

In the moonlight that lay across her bed, Susie saw something that looked like a stuffed animal. Had she forgotten to put one of her toys away? She picked it up and looked closely at it. It wasn't one of her toys. Had Mother bought her something new? She stroked its soft, soft fur. Just holding it made her feel less frightened.

Suddenly a quick, little voice said, "That's much better, Susie."

"Oh," squeaked Susie in fright as she threw the toy off the bed.

"Do you mind?" came a grumpy little voice from the floor. "I'm not a football, you know. My name is Valiant and I came here to help you. Pick me up, please, this instant."

Susie stared down at the little lump on the floor and grew very afraid indeed.

"I'm sorry!" said the mouse sharply. "But you can't be afraid of me. It's not on the list of things you're afraid of. It won't be permitted, you know."

"Are you sure?" asked Susie.

"Definitely!" Valiant replied. "Now please pick me up."

Susie got off her bed and ran across the cold floor. Stooping down, she picked up little Valiant.

"Oh!" he cried. "Not by my tail, if you please. Toys have feelings too, you know. Now you've got my ear! All right, All right. Now you're holding me correctly. Now where was I. Yes. My name is Valiant and I came here to help you."

"Help me do what?" said Susie, stroking his fur again.

"Mmmmmm," Valiant murmured. "Could you scratch just behind my left ear, while you're at it?"

Susie did, and Valiant giggled with delight. "Ah, that's wonderful, that's wonderful! I never can reach that spot."

At last Valiant stopped laughing and murmured happily again. Then he grew very quiet and Susie wondered if he had gone to sleep.

"Valiant," she whispered.

"Hunh? What?" answered Valiant sharply. "Ahem. Heh heh. Pardon me," he said, embarrassed. "I didn't come here just to have you scratch my ear, *did* I? No. As I said, I came to help you, Susie. To help you not be afraid of animals and lightning and thunder and your grandfather when he wears his glasses and especially of the dark."

"But I don't like the dark," said Susie.
"Why?"

"Because I can't see."

"Can't see what?"

"I don't know. I can't see them."

Valiant sighed. "We're not getting very far, are we? Okay. What do you *think* is out there in the dark?"

"Oh," said Susie. "Lions maybe. Or nasty people. Or green monsters with red eyes."

"Yes, yes, I see now," Valiant said. He sounded like Susie's doctor when he was about to say why Susie was sick. Only Valiant didn't say, "You have whatchamatosis," or anything like that. Instead he said, "You've been wearing your imagination eyes to bed, haven't you?"

"My imagination eyes?" asked Susie.

"Yep, imagination eyes. They'll do it every time. They're wonderful things to have around in the daytime when you're pretending and playing and all that. But in the dark? My goodness, there's no end to the trouble they can cause in the dark. You need to wear your real eyes to bed, Susie."

"What do you mean?" asked Susie.

"Here, I'll show you," Valiant replied. "Can you reach the light switch on the wall?"

"Of course, I can," said Susie. "I'm forty-eleven inches tall now." Then going to the switch with Valiant held snuggly under her arm, she flipped it on. "See?"

"Very good," declared Angel Valiant. "Now, tell me what you see hanging on the back of your door."

"My bathrobe," Susie answered.

"Excellent, excellent. Now turn off the light, please."

Susie obeyed, and the room grew dark again.

"Now, Susie," said the mouse. "Tell me what you see on the back of your door."

Susie looked at the black, humpy thing hanging there. "Oh!" she said. "It looks like a man. No. No. It's an elephant. No, it's a big old monster."

Her voice was getting higher and squeakier because she was getting more and more afraid.

"Hold it!" said Valiant. "You're wearing your imagination eyes again. What did your real eyes see just a minute ago on the door?"

"My bathrobe?" said Susie in a little, tiny voice.

"Your bathrobe," repeated Valiant. "You saw your bathrobe with your real eyes. It's a real thing and it won't change and become something else. Right?"

"I guess so," Susie said, stroking Valiant's fur. "But I'd feel better if you would stay with me anyway."

"I'll stay with you as long as you need me," said Valiant. "And I'll remind you to wear your real eyes whenever you're afraid. But do you think we could go to bed now and get some sleep?"

Susie opened her mouth in a big yawn and rubbed her eyes. "Okay," she said. Then she crawled into bed and held Valiant snuggled close to her heart. For a moment she felt a little frightened again. But then she stroked Valiant's fur and she felt better.

"Good night, Valiant," she said at last.

"Good night, Susie," murmured Valiant. Then, "Good night, all you Ark Angels up there," he added in a whisper. "Good night, Higher Ark. And good night, God. Sweet dreams."